Happy Birthday,
HELLO KITTY®

Abrams Books for Young Readers
New York

Hello Kitty was very excited, because the next day was her birthday!

As Mama tucked her into bed, Hello Kitty thought about her birthday and how much fun it would be to celebrate with all of her friends.

The next morning, Hello Kitty woke up bright and early.
In the kitchen, Mama was making a cake for her party.
It was going to be vanilla with banana cream in the middle
and chocolate frosting on top.

Hello Kitty asked Mama if she needed any help.
Mama said she could help stir the butter and cocoa
for the frosting. Don't forget to add the sugar!

Mimmy joined Mama and Hello Kitty in the kitchen to make cookies for the party.

After the cookies came out of the oven and cooled, Hello Kitty and Mimmy decorated them with sprinkles and frosting.

Hello Kitty looked at the list of things she needed to do before the guests arrived. She'd better get started. The party was supposed to begin in two hours.

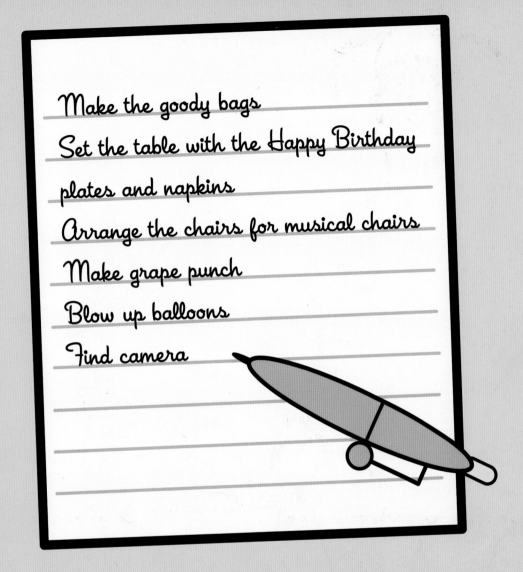

Make the goody bags

Set the table with the Happy Birthday plates and napkins

Arrange the chairs for musical chairs

Make grape punch

Blow up balloons

Find camera

Hello Kitty still needed to find her camera so she could take a picture of the party for Grandma and Grandpa White, who were on vacation in Florida. She added "Find camera" to her list of things to do.

Hello Kitty wanted to have beautiful flowers at her party,
so she went out to the garden to pick some.

Everything was in bloom! Hello Kitty picked a bouquet
of sunflowers and daisies for the table.

Hello Kitty was happy that Grandma and Grandpa were enjoying their vacation in Florida, but she really wished they could be at her party. She wondered what they were doing on their trip. Probably relaxing at the beach!

Mimmy also missed Grandma and Grandpa and
suggested that Hello Kitty make two extra goody
bags, just in case. She put bubbles, stickers, candy,
and star-shaped sunglasses in each one.

The goody bags were ready by the door. The table was all set. The chairs in the living room were gathered in the center for game time.

Mama and Mimmy blew up lots of blue, red, yellow, green, and purple balloons. It was time for the party!

Hello Kitty and Mimmy waited by the door for everyone to arrive. The doorbell rang! Who was the first guest?

It was Fifi, carrying a big present for Hello Kitty.
The box was almost bigger than Fifi!

Joey was the next to arrive, followed by Tracy and
Thomas, who had presents for Hello Kitty!

Dear Daniel, Tippy, and Jodie arrived shortly after.
Everyone was there and excited about the party.

Next it was time for cake and ice cream. Everyone sang "Happy Birthday" to Hello Kitty, and then it was time to make a wish. What should she wish for? Hello Kitty thought about Grandma and Grandpa and then closed her eyes and blew out all the candles.

As everyone enjoyed cake and ice cream cones, Hello Kitty opened her presents. She got a teddy bear, a shiny red wagon, and a new soccer ball. What wonderful gifts! She was very grateful to all of her nice friends.

Time for a picture! Mama gathered everyone together and told them, "Say cheese!" Hello Kitty would show it to Grandma and Grandpa when they got back from their trip.

Suddenly, the doorbell rang. Who could it be? Everyone was already there. Hello Kitty opened the door and saw Grandma and Grandpa. They had come home early to surprise her! This was the best present of all.

Library of Congress Cataloging-in-Publication Data

Happy birthday, Hello Kitty / Sanrio Co., LTD.
pages cm
Summary: "It's Hello Kitty's birthday, and she's inviting all her friends over for
a party to celebrate. Mama is making a cake, Mimmy is setting up the game,
and Papa is getting the balloons. Be there with Hello Kitty as she plans her
party, opens presents, spends time with friends, blows out her candles,
and makes a wish"— Provided by publisher.
ISBN 978-1-4197-1466-5 (paperback)
I. Sanrio, Kabushiki Kaisha.
PZ7.H19977 2014
[E]—dc23
2014012550

Printed and bound in China
10 9 8 7 6 5 4 3 2 1

Abrams Books for Young Readers are available at special discounts when
purchased in quantity for premiums and promotions as well as fundraising or
educational use. Special editions can also be created to specification.
For details, contact specialsales@abramsbooks.com or the address below.

THE ART OF BOOKS SINCE 1949

115 West 18th Street
New York, NY 10011
www.abramsbooks.com